Max and Zoe

at Soccer Practice

by Shelley Swanson Sateren

illustrated by Mary Sullivan

PICTURE WINDOW BOOKS
a capstone imprint

Max and Zoe is published by Picture Window Books
a Capstone Imprint
1710 Roe Crest Drive
North Mankato, Minnesota 56003
www.capstonepub.com

Library of Congress Cataloging-in-Publication Data
Sateren, Shelley Swanson.
  Max and Zoe at soccer practice / by Shelley Swanson Sateren ;
illustrated by Mary Sullivan.
    p. cm. -- (Max and Zoe)
  Summary: Max and Zoe cooperate to improve both their soccer
skills.
  ISBN 978-1-4048-6213-5 (library binding)
  1. Best friends--Juvenile fiction. 2. Cooperativeness--Juvenile
fiction. 3. Soccer stories. [1. Soccer--Fiction. 2. Best friends--
Fiction. 3. Friendship--Fiction. 4. Cooperativeness--Fiction.]
I. Sullivan, Mary, 1958- ill. II. Title. III. Series: Sateren, Shelley
Swanson. Max and Zoe.

PZ7.S249155Maq 2012
813.54--dc23

                          2011051237

Designer: Emily Harris

Printed in the United States of America in Stevens Point, Wisconsin.
032013   007240R

Table of Contents

It was Saturday, and the first soccer practice of the season had begun. Max and Zoe were excited.

"Wow, Max," said Zoe. "You're so good at dribbling. I stink at it!"

5

"You're not that bad, Zoe. You only bumped over five cones," Max said.

Zoe frowned. "There are only five cones in this drill, Max."

"Okay, team," called Coach. "Line up for toe touches!"

Zoe watched as Max did the drill perfectly. During her turn, Zoe's foot slid off the top of the ball. She fell onto the grass.

"You are the best at everything, Max," Zoe said with a sigh.

"No, I'm not," Max replied.

"You do the best round-offs. You're the fastest reader. And you're the best at soccer," Zoe said.

"Well, you do the longest headstands, and you're way better at math," Max said.

"I guess," Zoe said.

Coach blew his whistle again. "Time for running drills!" he said.

"At least I'm good at running," Zoe said.

"I'm not," said Max. "I'm always the last one."

Zoe and Max lined up for the running drill.

"Ready, set, GO!" Coach yelled.

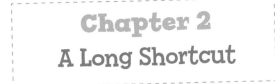

Chapter 2
A Long Shortcut

Max ran hard. He had to keep up with Zoe.

Coach had told them to run all of the way around the field. It was really far!

Max was sweating, and his legs were really tired. Worst of all, he was in last place.

Zoe led the pack. She sped past the first goal. Max ran toward it, too.

Coach had said, "No
cutting in front of the goals."

But Max was so tired. And
he hated being last.

He looked over his
shoulder. Coach wasn't
looking. This was his chance.

Max ran in front of the goal. He caught up to the other runners.

"Hey, you cheated!" yelled a boy behind him.

The race ended. The boy

who came in last told the

coach that Max cheated.

"Is that true, Max?" asked

Coach.

Max kicked the dirt. "Yes.

I didn't want to be last,"

he said.

"Shortcuts don't work,
Max," said Coach. "The
only way to get better is to
practice. Run another lap."

Max did, all by himself.

"I wish I was a good
runner," he thought.

"Game time!" called

Coach.

Everyone chased after the

ball. Max couldn't keep up.

He didn't kick the ball once.

He was too tired.

After practice, Max went

to Zoe's house.

"I'm going to quit soccer,"

Max said.

"Don't quit," Zoe begged.

"You're really good at

dribbling and toe touches."

"Well, if I could run like you, maybe I'd stay," he said.

"I can run, but I can't do the other stuff," she said.

Max thought for a minute. "How about you help me, and I'll help you?"

"Good idea! We'll be way better by next Saturday," Zoe said as she gave Max a high five.

So Max and Zoe ran races

and practiced dribbling.

They worked hard every day.

They did lots of different

drills. Sometimes they put

toys all over the yard and

ran around them.

By Friday, Max ran faster

and breathed easier. Zoe

was able to do toe touches

without falling.

On Saturday at practice,

Coach said, "Better running,

Max! Better dribbling, Zoe!"

"Let's keep practicing at home, okay?" whispered Max.

"Yeah. We'll do better than better. We'll be the best!" Zoe whispered back.

"Pretty soon we'll be soccer stars, Zoe! Race you across the field," Max said.

"You're on, Max!" Zoe said.

About the Author

Shelley Swanson Sateren is the author of many children's books and has worked as an editor and a bookseller. Today, besides writing, she works with children aged five to twelve in an after-school program. At home or at the cabin, Shelley loves to read, watch movies, cross-country ski, and walk. She lives in St. Paul, Minnesota, with her husband and two sons.

About the Illustrator

Mary Sullivan has been drawing and writing her whole life, which has mostly been spent in Texas. She earned her BFA from the University of Texas in Studio Art, but she considers herself a self-trained illustrator. Mary lives in Cedar Park, a suburb of Austin, Texas.

Glossary

cheated (CHEET-ed) — to act without being honest, in order to win a game or get what you want

dribble (DRIB-uhl) — to move a ball while running, keeping it under your control

goal (GOHL) — a frame with a net into which you aim a soccer ball

headstand (HED-stand) — the act of holding yourself upright on your head with the help of your hands

round-off (ROUND-awf) — an act like a cartwheel that ends with both legs together at the same time, facing backward from where you started

shortcut (SHORT-kut) — a shorter or quicker way

Discussion Questions

1. Max cheated during the running drill. His coach made him run another lap. Do you think the coach's punishment was fair? Why or why not?

2. Have you ever cheated or wanted to cheat? Discuss your answer.

3. Max wasn't good at running, so he wanted to quit soccer. Have you ever wanted to quit something that was hard for you? Explain your answer.

Writing Prompts

1. Think about something you want to get better at. Make a list of three things you can do to make that happen.

2. Max and Zoe helped each other become better soccer players. Write about a time when you helped a friend.

3. Max and Zoe like soccer. Write three sentences about your favorite activity.

Soccer Drills

Zoe and Max made up their own drills to get better at soccer. You can do your own drills, too!

What you need:

- a safe space for running, such as a yard
- two soccer balls or two stuffed animals
- a tape measure
- a timer
- paper
- pencil or pen

What you do:

1. Put one ball or stuffed animal at one end of your yard. With the tape measure, measure out 15 feet. Put the second ball or animal at the other end.

2. Jog at a slow speed between the two balls or animals. Jog back and forth five times.

3. Next, raise your knees high when you run. Run back and forth five times. Now you are warmed up.

4. Now have a friend time you as you run as fast as you can between the balls or animals. Speed back and forth five times.

5. Record your time so you can see how you improve each time you do this drill.

6. When you finish, be sure to rest and drink some water.

The Fun Doesn't Stop Here!

Discover more at www.capstonekids.com

- Videos & Contests
- Games & Puzzles
- Friends & Favorites
- Authors & Illustrators